Deputy Dorkface

How Mannerland Got Its Manners Back

Second Printing

No portion of this book may be reproduced in any form or by
any means without permission in writing from the publisher,
except for the inclusion of brief quotations in a review.

Art direction/design, & editing: Sue Campbell
Illustration: Eldon Doty

Cataloging in Publication

Janison, Kevin D.

Deputy Dorkface : how Mannerland got its manners back /
Kevin D. Janison ; illustrated by Eldon Doty.

32 p. : ill. ; 30 cm.

ISBN: 1-935043-47-1
ISBN-13: 978-1-935043-47-8

After the children of Mannerland suddenly lose all their
manners, Deputy Dorkface decides he must help the
community to regain those manners.

1. Etiquette for children and teenagers—Fiction. 2. Courtesy—
Fiction. I. Title. II. Doty, Eldon.

[E] dc22   2011   2010942726

STEPHENS PRESS
A Stephens Media Company

P.O. Box 371153
Las Vegas, Nevada 89134

www.DeputyDorkface.com

To buy books:
http://deputydorkface.com/buy-the-books/
*To arrange for Kevin Janison to speak at your school or group,
send email to:* info@DeputyDorkface.com

Printed in China

Production Date: 10.10.14
Plant&Location:Printed by Everbest Printing(Guangzhou,China),Co.Ltd
Job/Batch# 701930

Dedication

To the students and teachers of
Lummis Elementary School:
for your ears, eyes, and laughter.
Thank you for helping the adventures
of Deputy Dorkface evolve.

Once upon a time in the small town of Mannerland, a suburb of the Metropolis of Mannertopia, a strange storm passed through, leaving the children ill-mannered and their parents confounded.

Mannerland had prided itself on the fine manners of its people, generation after generation.

On that summer day, a strange wind began to blow in dark, threatening clouds with lightning and thunder. Mannerland had never seen anything like it, because in Mannertopia even the weather was always well-behaved.

From his motorcycle, Deputy Dorkface watched the wild storm. He was stunned when a bolt of lightning hit the "Welcome to Mannerland" sign. It sliced the "Manner" clean off—leaving only "land" behind.

"Uh oh! This is not a good sign!" said Deputy Dorkface.

He was right. From that day forward the children changed. Bad manners spread quickly through the community.

"I will not clean my room!" Katie screamed. Instead, she stuffed her clothes, toys, and her little brother under her bed.

"I can talk with my mouth full if I want to!" shouted David, while spraying his mom with half-mashed peas.

Ellie said to her mom, "Yo lady! Gimme some breakfast."

The children forgot about *please* and *thank you*. It was *gimme that*, and *I'll do what I want*. They forgot about sharing, kindness, and the feelings of others. They cut in line, stopped holding the door open for others, and who needs a tissue to wipe your nose when you can use your sleeve, or your friend's sleeve?

"I've got to do something!" proclaimed Deputy Dorkface.

The deputy rushed through the radio station door and stopped a popular song right in the middle. He grabbed the microphone and announced:

"This is Deputy Dorkface. Since the storm, our young Mannerlanders have completely lost their good manners. This is horrible. We can no longer be called 'Mannerland.' As your town official, I am officially changing the name of our city effective today. From this day forthwith, I hereby rename this town, 'Land'."

"Manners are gone forever?" asked Mr. Flynn.
"Cool!" shouted the twins, Billie and Lilly.
They threw their food at the wall just to see the
explosions. They jumped on the furniture, had a pillow
fight, then swung from the fan and burped.

Deputy Dorkface made his way to the town square. A large group of parents gathered next to the Manners Magnetron. The device flashed lights and rang bells—detecting manners violations all over town.

"What would you like me to do?"

The parents shouted all at once. No one waited politely for their turn.

"Don't give up on our kids!"

"How can we get these kids to behave?"

"My kid talks back to me!"

"We need help fast!"

MANNERS MAGNETRON

Interrupting	385
Talking with Mouth Full	221
Inconsiderate	1543
Nose Picking	845
Rude Dudes	144

ALert Status 9

POLITE IS RIGHT!

Hi, Mom

I WANT MY OLD KIDS BACK!

My kids burp at the dinner table!

Grandchildren FOR SALE

My puppies are better trained!

"Calm down. Sshhh. Let me think," said the deputy.

Nothing the parents tried worked—grounding the kids, taking away cell phones, restricting TV time—none of the usual punishments made the kids behave well and rewards only made them worse.

"Can you pleeeeeeease help us?" prodded an exasperated teacher.

After what seemed like forever, but was only ten minutes, the deputy looked up and smiled. "I have an idea!"

13

Deputy Dorkface explained his plan to the parents.

"So you see, we'll build it here in the square and we'll invite the kids to take part in a TV reality show!"

"Can that work?" asked several skeptical parents.

"It couldn't hurt," said another.

So the parents set to work that night while their children stayed home messing up their rooms, watching the late, late, late show, coughing without covering, and whining about doing homework.

They had no clue what was coming.

The next school day, the kids' bad manners hit new highs. They interrupted their teachers, nose picked, and made disgusting noises. They sneezed in their hands and then high-fived their friends. They cut in line, cheated in games, and the lunch lady had to dodge the flying grilled cheese sandwiches.

Their behavior was so bad the teachers ran screaming from the school!

While the kids raised havoc in school, their parents worked on the *Good Manners Manor* set. It looked just like the real town, but smaller. They:

sawed lumber,

hammered nails,

painted walls, and

by late that night,

Good Manners Manor was ready.

The next day, Deputy Dorkface made an announcement on the school's
TV station, but the rowdy kids couldn't hear it. Frustrated, he rang the bell.

R r r r r r r innnnng!

    R r r r r r r innnnng!

They still didn't hear. So he tried the buzzer that sounds like a donkey.

E e e e A w w w Buzzzzzzzzz!

    E e e e A w w w Buzzzzzzzzz!

And finally, both at once!

E e e e A w w w Buzzzzzzzzz! R r r r r r r innnnng!

    E e e e A w w w Buzzzzzzzzz! R r r r r r r innnnng!

That got the kids' attention.

"Good morning young ladies and gentlemen. This is Deputy Dorkface. On behalf of your fine parents and Channel Nine Nice News, I invite students to take part in a new reality show!"

"We'll be on TV!" Ellie shouted happily.

But the deputy wasn't finished.

"One more thing … for the week of filming, there will be no school."

"H U R R A Y !" The shouts could be heard for miles.

That afternoon, the kids joyously entered the gates of *Good Manners Manor*, but the gates slammed shut behind them!

"Now remember, this is YOUR town. YOU decide proper behavior. YOU make the rules. Then the deputy and the grownups turned around and went home, not mentioning that TV cameras were filming their every move.

"We're in charge?" asked Anna.

"It's OUR TOWN!" shouted David, "We can do what we want."

For a moment everyone froze, then …

"Let's play!" yelled the children, as they scattered off in separate directions.

—Land grew very quiet. For the next three days, the children did as they pleased. They chewed with open mouths, slammed doors, gossiped, and called each other names. Nobody took turns, and big kids put little kids in trash cans. By the fourth day, kids woke up in the smelly, dirty *Manor*. They waded through the mess and looked around at each other. They had hurt feelings, matted and tangled hair, and snotty noses. Yuck!

"Look at us, we're gross! I wanna go home to my nice clean house, where people are nice to me and I am nice to them," cried Lilly.

"I wanna go home too! Please?" Katie begged into the TV camera.

In the homes of —Land, the appalled parents watched *Good Manners Manor* on TV. When the kids cried on camera, the parents were ready to pick them up.

Deputy Dorkface watched the mayhem in the *Manor* and smiled.

When the parents called his office he was ready.

"We'd like our children home, please!" called a mother.

"But not like they are now," said a father, "they are more bad-mannered than ever!"

"Not so fast!" replied the deputy.

Deputy Dorkface explained the **Manners Matchup** to the parents. The kids would have to earn their way home.

Three kids and three parents faced off in a contest of good manners. Most of –Land's residents had gathered in the square to watch it live. It was kids versus parents!

Round one: table manners.

Mrs. Shelby and David sat with plates of spaghetti. Mrs. Shelby draped her napkin across her lap and then carefully twirled a small bite of noodles around her fork, neatly delivering it to her mouth. She chewed quietly with her mouth closed, and then dabbed her lips with the napkin. She sat back and smiled across the table at David.

David gave his plate a hard look, pushed the fork and napkin to the floor, and dove in face first, wolfing down the food like a hungry Saint Bernard. Noodles and sauce flew as he lifted his smeared face and sucked down the last noodle with a loud S L U R P !

Buz z z z z z z z z z !

Score: Parents–1 Kids–0

Round two: sharing.

Deputy Dorkface presented one package of delicious chocolate chip cookies each to Mr. Flynn and Ellie.

Ellie took the cookies over to the other children, offering the cookies to all. Each child took a cookie and then Ellie helped herself to one. But Mr. Flynn stuck the bag of cookies inside his coat, hiding them from the other parents. He turned and grinned to his team, who saw that he'd hogged the cookies. They ran over and tackled him and grabbed for the treats, yelling, "Gimme one!"

Buz z z z z z z z z z z z! Buz z z z z z z z z z z z! End of round two.

Score: Parents–1 Kids–1 The match is tied!

A hush fell all over –Land. The mood was tense.

Katie faced off against her mom to break the tie. As soon as the Deputy started to explain the contest, Katie interrupted him and gushed, "Oh my gosh, are we on TV too?"

Her mother waited patiently for instructions.

"Yes, you're on TV," said Deputy Dorkface. He continued, "Now here's what we're …"

"Oh my gosh! Hee hee hee … how's my hair?" exclaimed Katie, not waiting for Deputy Dorkface to finish. She then grabbed the fork from the spaghetti contest to comb her bangs.

The buzzer buzzed loudly: *Buz z z z z z z z z z z* !

Score: Parents–2 Kids–1 The parents win!!

The parents went wild!

They yelled, "We're number one! They waggled their tongues and even shook their behinds at the kids. The kids were embarrassed and ashamed of the parents' behavior.

Deputy Dorkface buzzed the buzzer, *Buz z z z z z z z z z ! Buz z z z z z z z z !* to try to make them stop. He grabbed the microphone and announced, "Ladies and gentlemen, puhleeze! I am shocked. Good sportsmanship is always important whether you win or lose. Because of your bad manners, I must deduct points."

The parents stopped cheering.

"Therefore, the overall winners of the **Manners Matchup** are the children of Mannerland! Kids, you're free to go home!"

The kids and adults cheered! Then the children, in a display of good sportsmanship, shook hands with the team of grownups.

Afterward, they all walked home together.

So, the town got its whole name, and its manners back.

From that day on, the kids (and the parents) of Mannerland found that being polite really wasn't hard at all. In fact, Anna and a group of kids went to the town hall to give Deputy Dorkface special thanks.

"Thank you for teaching us good manners, sir."

"You're welcome, Anna," the deputy replied.

"Thanks for 'welcoming' my thanks," she said.

"No problem at all," he said and grinned.

"Thank you for saying it's no problem."

"Uh, you're welcome?" said a confused Deputy Dorkface.

"Thanks for the welcoming to my thanking you for the previous 'you're welcome,' for thanking you the first time," Anna said with a big smile.

The Deputy tipped his hat, and then ran back to his office in search of another plan.